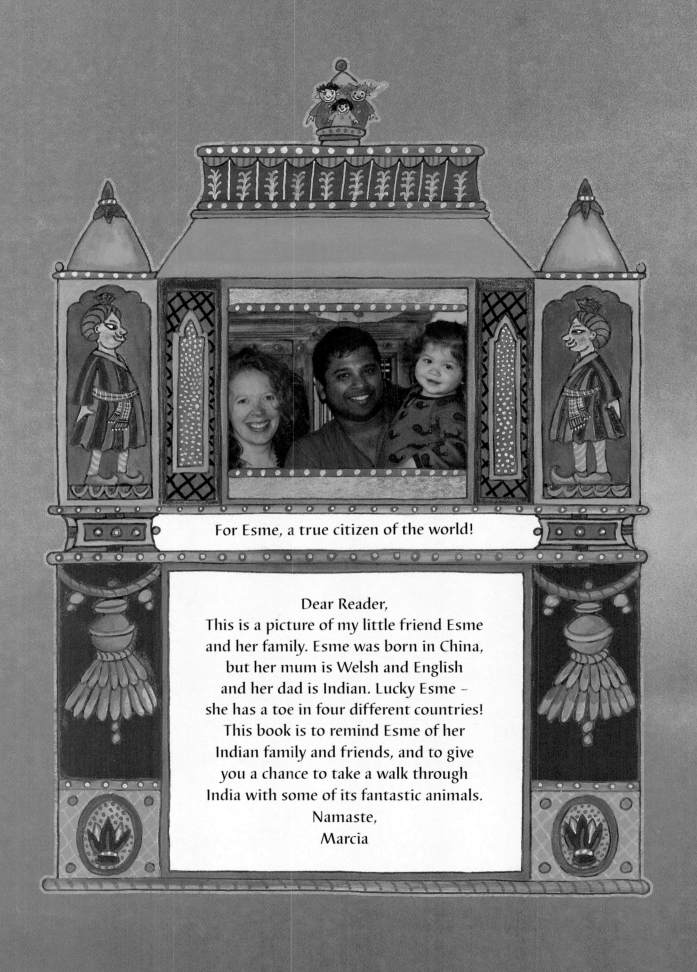

For Esme, a true citizen of the world!

Dear Reader,
This is a picture of my little friend Esme
and her family. Esme was born in China,
but her mum is Welsh and English
and her dad is Indian. Lucky Esme –
she has a toe in four different countries!
This book is to remind Esme of her
Indian family and friends, and to give
you a chance to take a walk through
India with some of its fantastic animals.
Namaste,
Marcia

The Elephant's Friend
and
Other Tales
from
Ancient India

Retold and illustrated by
Marcia Williams

WALKER BOOKS
AND SUBSIDIARIES
LONDON · BOSTON · SYDNEY · AUCKLAND

The Elephant's Friend

Once upon a time there was an elephant that lived in the palace stables.

He was the king's favourite elephant, so he was always well fed and cared for.

Outside the palace walls a dog lay in the dirt – uncared for and starving.

He could smell the rice fed to the elephant and his poor tummy rumbled.

One lucky day, the dog managed to slip through the palace gates.
Once inside, he followed the scent of the warm rice to the elephant's stable.

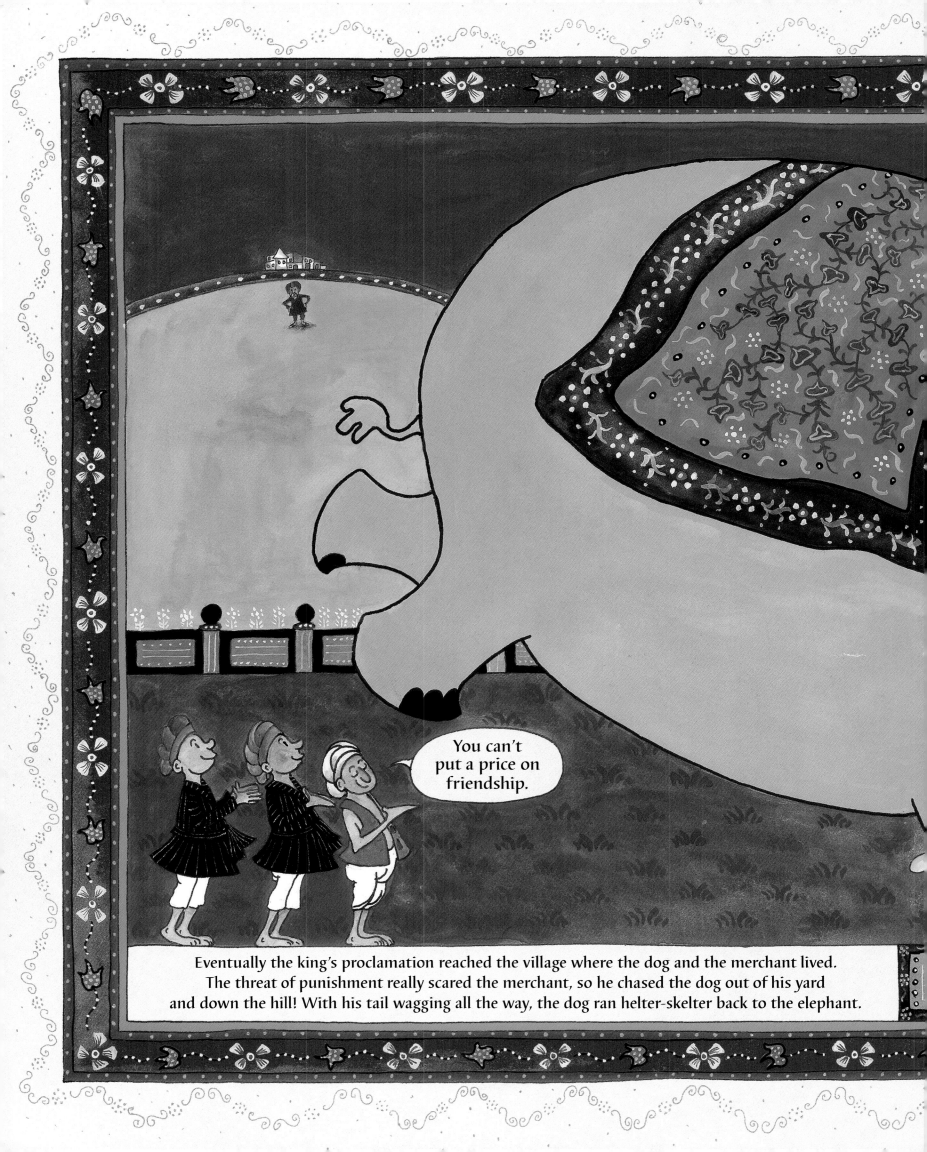

Eventually the king's proclamation reached the village where the dog and the merchant lived. The threat of punishment really scared the merchant, so he chased the dog out of his yard and down the hill! With his tail wagging all the way, the dog ran helter-skelter back to the elephant.

The elephant and the dog danced with delight while the king, his ministers and the elephant's keeper all cheered and clapped. And so the two friends lived contentedly together for the rest of their days and nobody, but nobody, ever tried to part them again!

The Scrawny Old Tiger

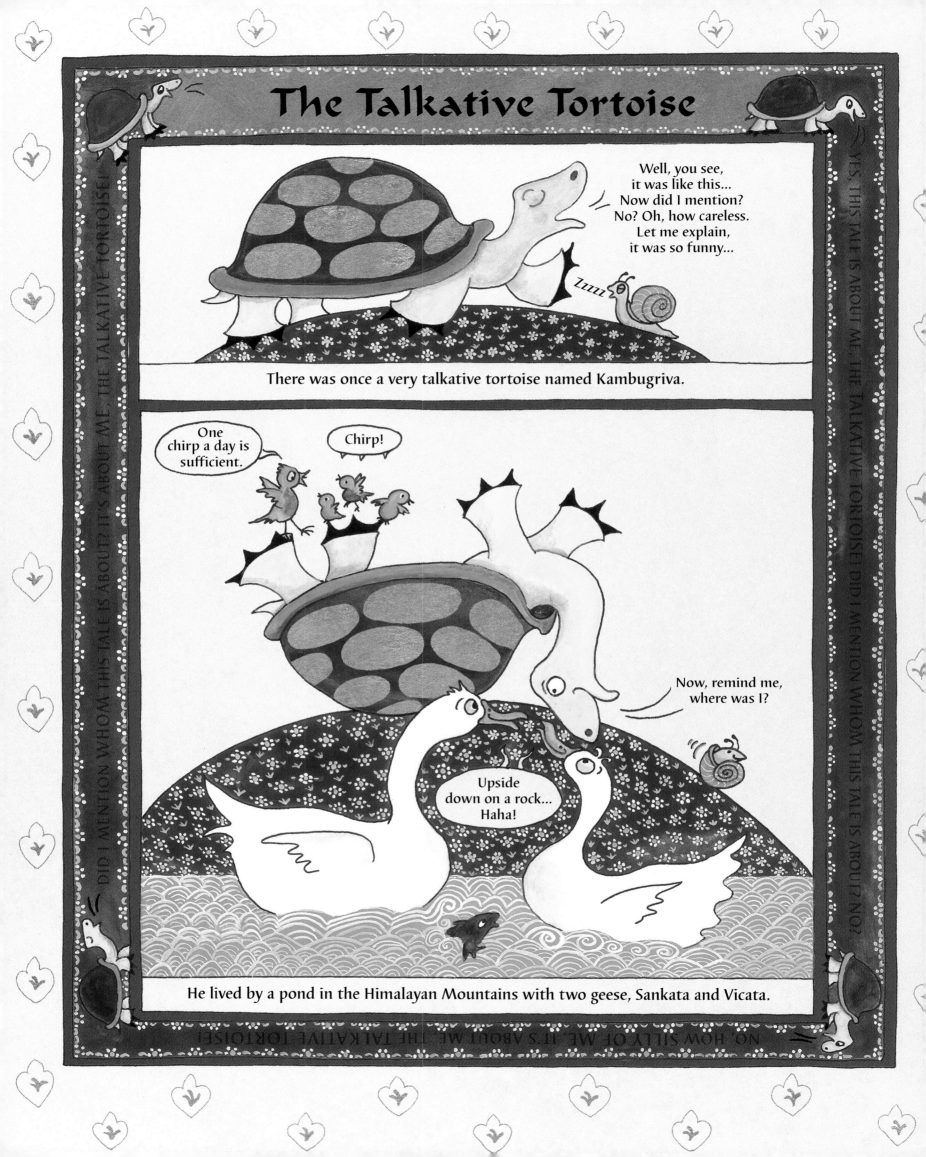

The Talkative Tortoise

There was once a very talkative tortoise named Kambugriva.

He lived by a pond in the Himalayan Mountains with two geese, Sankata and Vicata.

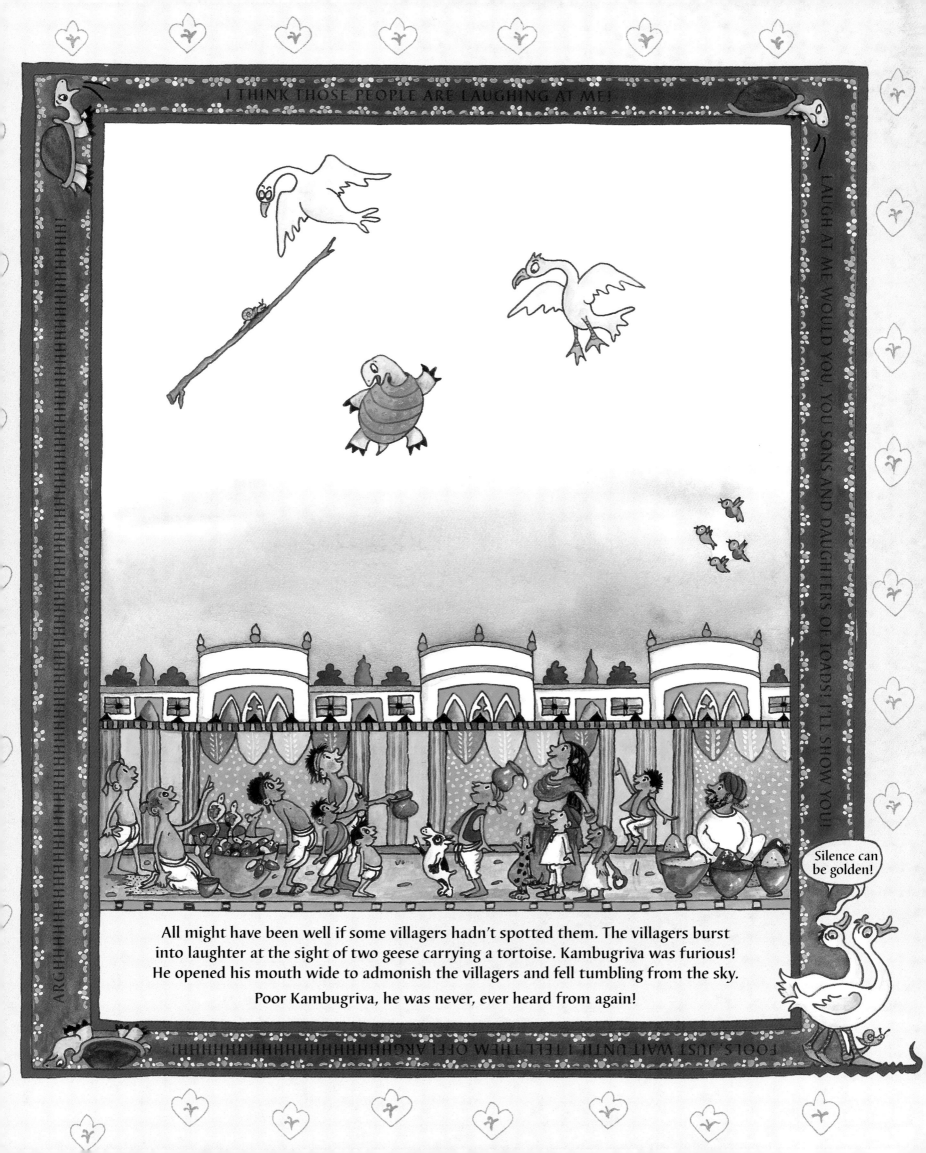

All might have been well if some villagers hadn't spotted them. The villagers burst into laughter at the sight of two geese carrying a tortoise. Kambugriva was furious! He opened his mouth wide to admonish the villagers and fell tumbling from the sky.

Poor Kambugriva, he was never, ever heard from again!

The Wise Little Pebet

The Golden Swan

Once upon a time there was a swan with feathers made of the purest gold.
The swan lived on a fine pond and was rich in both food and friends.

Close by the pond there lived a poor mother with her two daughters.
Their clothes were rags, their food meagre and their luxuries non-existent.

The swan felt sad that they had so little and he had so much.

The mother and her daughters gasped in horror, but it was too late. The swan took his leave of the ungrateful woman, who had returned his generosity with such greed. He went with his friends to live in a far distant land, never to return to the little shack again.

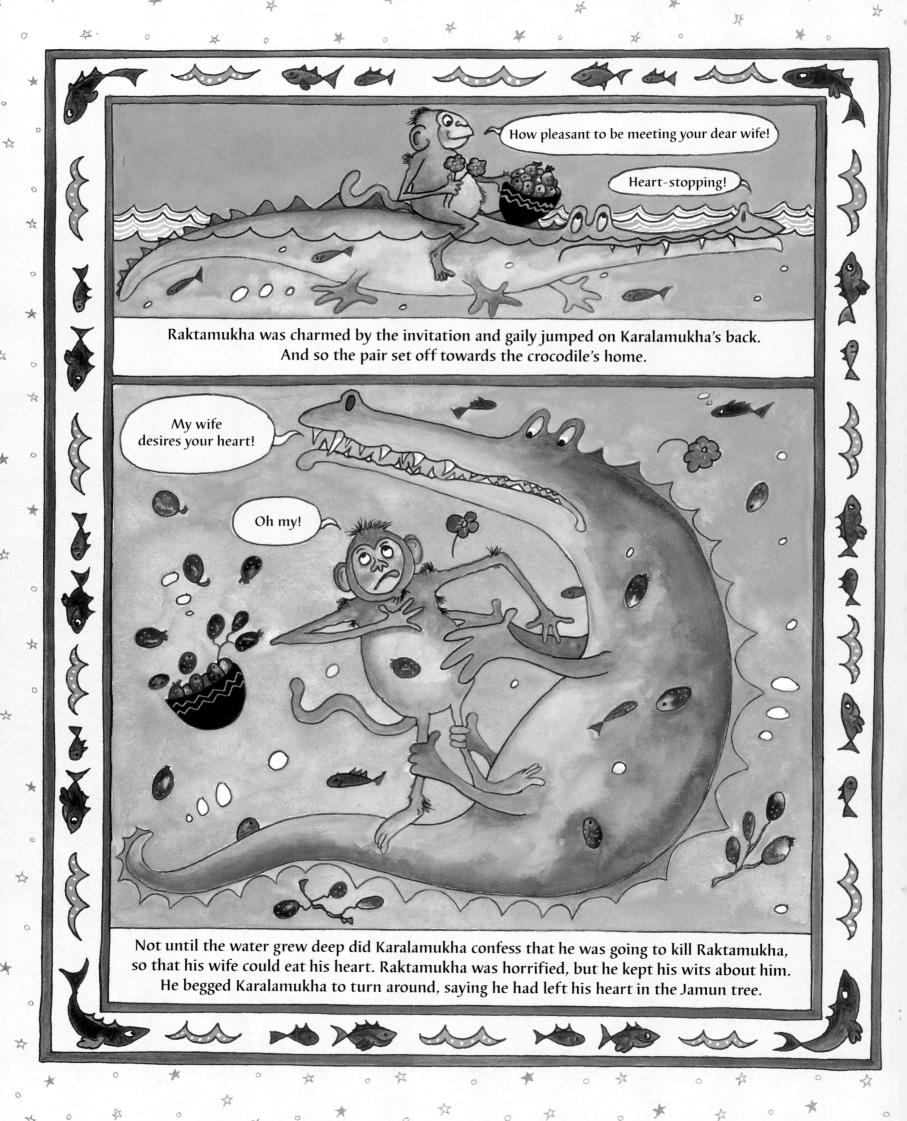

Raktamukha was charmed by the invitation and gaily jumped on Karalamukha's back.
And so the pair set off towards the crocodile's home.

Not until the water grew deep did Karalamukha confess that he was going to kill Raktamukha,
so that his wife could eat his heart. Raktamukha was horrified, but he kept his wits about him.
He begged Karalamukha to turn around, saying he had left his heart in the Jamun tree.

The Tale of the Three Large Fish

Once upon a watery time there lived three large fish.
One was wise, one was clever and the other believed in fate!

The three fish were good friends and always swam about together.
Until the day they overheard two fishermen planning to cast their net into the lake.

The wise fish begged his two friends to leave the lake,
or they might be caught in the net.

However, his two friends preferred to take their chances in the lake,
so the wise fish left on his own.

The very next day the fish that believed in fate was caught in the net
of the fishermen and that was the end of him!

The clever fish was also caught in the net. However, being clever, he pretended to be dead. So the
fishermen cast him back into the lake. There he lived for the rest of his large, clever and rather lonely life!

The Foolish Lion

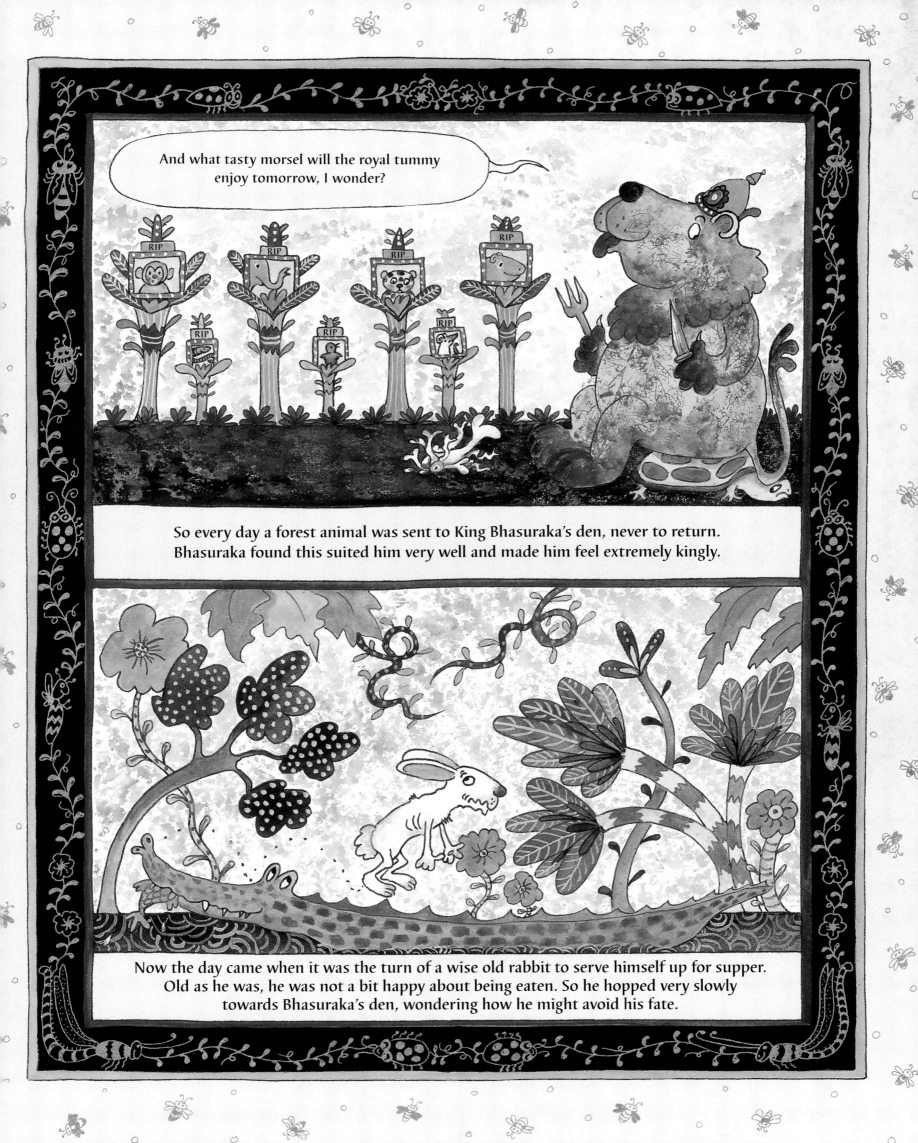

So every day a forest animal was sent to King Bhasuraka's den, never to return. Bhasuraka found this suited him very well and made him feel extremely kingly.

Now the day came when it was the turn of a wise old rabbit to serve himself up for supper. Old as he was, he was not a bit happy about being eaten. So he hopped very slowly towards Bhasuraka's den, wondering how he might avoid his fate.

By the time Wise Old Rabbit reached the lion's den, Bhasuraka was roaring with impatience. When he saw the skinny old rabbit appear he roared even louder!

Wise Old Rabbit apologized profusely for his lateness and his smallness. He explained that he had set out with five companions but another lion, who also claimed to be king of the forest, had eaten them. When King Bhasuraka heard this he almost exploded and swore to tear the impostor to shreds!

So Wise Old Rabbit led Bhasuraka down a forest path to a well, where he said the lion was hiding.

Bhasuraka looked down into the depths of the well and there he saw... a lion!

With his claws at the ready, Bhasuraka gave one mighty roar and leapt down the well towards the lion. Just seconds before he hit the water and drowned, Bhasuraka realized that he was jumping towards his own reflection.

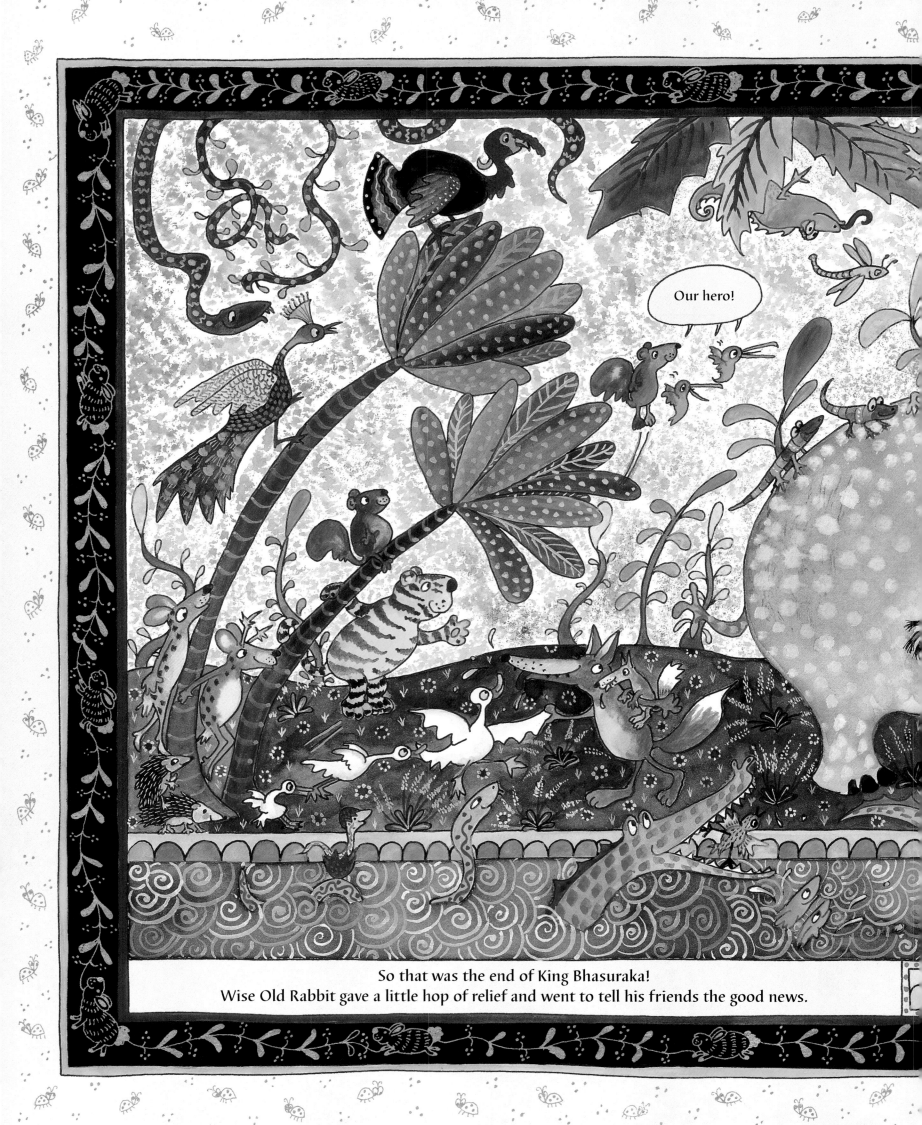

So that was the end of King Bhasuraka!
Wise Old Rabbit gave a little hop of relief and went to tell his friends the good news.

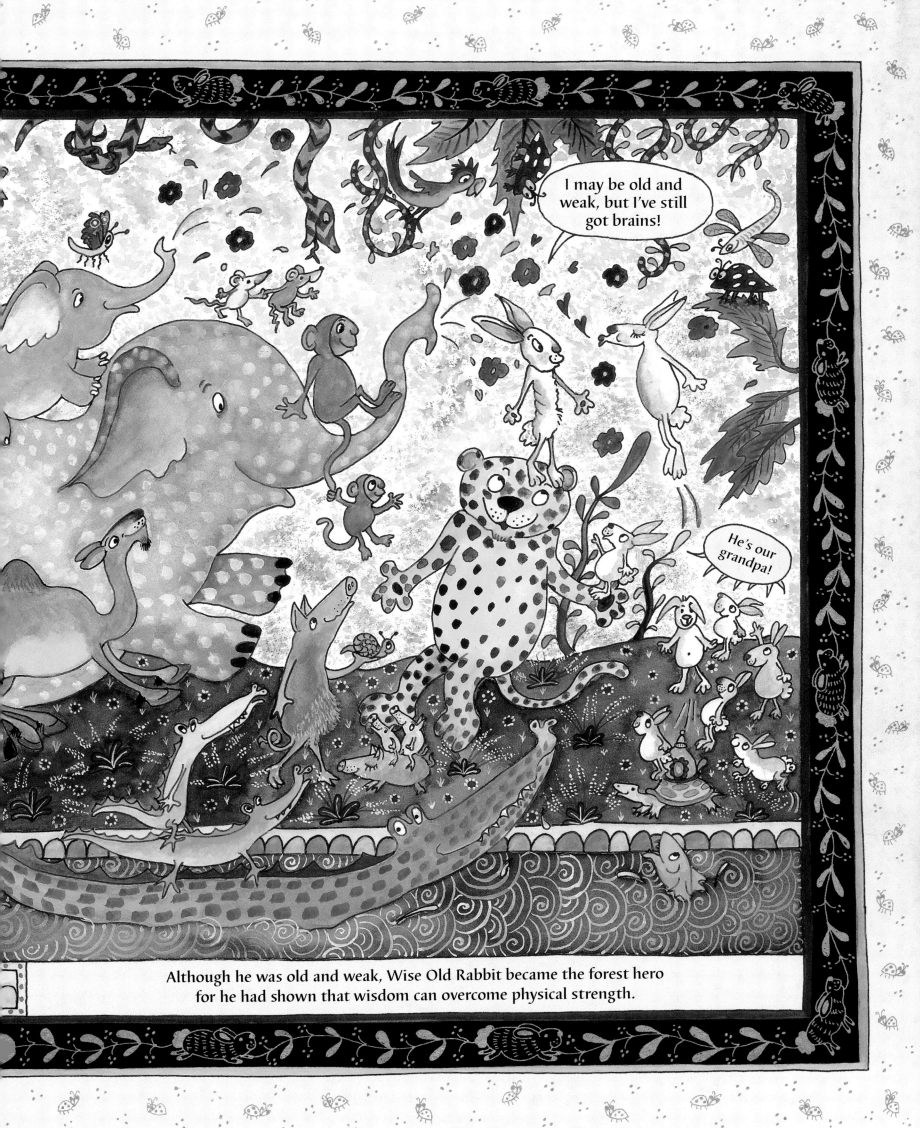

Although he was old and weak, Wise Old Rabbit became the forest hero
for he had shown that wisdom can overcome physical strength.

First published 2012 by Walker Books Ltd
87 Vauxhall Walk, London SE11 5HJ

2 4 6 8 10 9 7 5 3 1

This book has been typeset in Barbedor and Ondine
Handlettering by Kate Slater

Printed in China

British Library Cataloguing in Publication Data:
a catalogue record for this book
is available from the British Library

ISBN 978-1-4063-3523-1

www.walker.co.uk

www.marciawilliams.co.uk